YOU ARE SOMETHING SPECIAL!

Inspiring and Motivational Stories about Love,

Gratitude and Mindfulness

(Present for Girls and Boys)

Annabelle Lindgreen

This book belongs to _____

Contents

At the end of the day, the boy and the men of the village went up to the field to get the sheep back to the farm for the night, but every single one had vanished.

Foreword

First and foremost, I hope more than anything that you enjoy the stories that are kept between the following pages and chapters. I'm a firm believer that stories are what make us human, their messages can span years, decades, and even centuries, and even now, we can tell stories to each other that have been around in our cultures and societies for thousands of years.

Just take a moment to process that. Stories people were telling each other thousands of years ago are still being told today. It blows my mind.

Continuing on with this frame of mind, I hope that the following stories will do the same or will at least make you smile or help you to see life in a new, beautiful, and mindful way. Some of these stories from this collection are retellings of classic stories that I was told as a child. Some are inspired by stories written by some of our time's greatest authors, and some you won't have read anywhere else.

With stunning words and gorgeous illustrations, get ready to get lost in some captivating worlds and magic.

So settle in, get your pyjamas on, pull up the duvet, get snuggled up in bed, and let's dive into some beautiful stories you and your children are going to love.

Story One – The Sad Swan

Once upon a time, there lived a swan who was easily the most beautiful swan anybody had ever seen. Every morning, the swan would plod on down to the nearby river and spend hours gazing into the still waters, admiring his own reflection.

"Wow. I am so beautiful," he would say to himself. "Is there anyone there who is as beautiful as me?"

Every morning, at the same time the swan went down to the river, the fish would swim over, each one stopping in awe to admire the swan and his beauty.

"Wow," the fish would say. "You are the most beautiful swan we've ever seen!"

The swan would smile to himself, then ask the fish to move along, hoping more fish would come along and see him for how beautiful he was. All the animals in the area agreed that this swan was the most beautiful.

One day, however, a voice in the swan's head started to ask the questions.

"Hello swan," said the voice in the swan's head, "Have you ever wondered that you might not be the most beautiful swan in the world?"

The swan walked over to the waters to admire himself. He was still beautiful, so no, he did not wonder.

"No, you see," the swan said, "I can see myself right now, and I am surely the most beautiful swan."

"Are you?" the voice replied. "Have you traveled all the lands and seen all the other swans? How can you be sure you're the most beautiful?"

The swan thought about this for a little while. He had not seen all the swans in all the land. He had not even traveled away from this river at any point in his life, so how could he be sure?

"What makes you so beautiful?" the voice in the swan's head asked.

"Well. My feathers are so clean and white, and my beak is so orange and pure. I am perfect in every way." The swan said proudly, trying to make himself seem happier. Still, instead, he was worrying so much that he might not be the most beautiful. It was strange for the swan to feel this way.

"Listen," the voice in the swan's head said.

The swan listened. At first, the swan could hear only his own thoughts. The voice told him he was so beautiful. The swan listened harder, listening through the voice in his head, and his thoughts went quiet. All he could hear was silence.

The swan listened harder still, and there, from the tree on the other side of the river, the swan heard the most beautiful bird song the swan had ever heard. It whistled and whooped and sang, and the song the bird was singing was so beautiful, it bought tears to the swan's eyes.

"Wow. That song is the most beautiful song I've ever heard," the swan said.

"You see," said the voice in the swan's head, "how can you be the most beautiful when that bird has the most beautiful voice?" And then the voice left.

The swan was incredibly sad for days, left thinking he was not the most beautiful and that his life might have been a lie. The fish still came by to admire the swan in the mornings, but the swan wasn't there. He was curled up under a tree. He didn't want to speak to anyone or see anyone unless he was the most beautiful. And still, every morning, the bird in the tree sang his beautiful song.

One morning, a rabbit hopped across the grass by the river and saw the swan being sad under the tree.

"Hey, swan. What is the matter?" the rabbit asked. "Why are you so sad?"

"Listen to that bird singing!" The swan cried. "I will never be able to sing in such a beautiful voice, so I must be ugly. I stay here under this tree, so nobody has to see me."

Now, this rabbit was a wise rabbit and had seen many things during his travels, and to help make the swan feel better, he shared some of his wisdom.

"Mr. Swan. You have no reason to be sad. You see, every living thing is beautiful in its own special way. While this bird has the most beautiful voice, you have the most beautiful feathers and the most orange beak I've ever seen. I, a rabbit, do not have a beautiful voice or beautiful feathers, but I have beautiful ears and soft fur."

The swan stood up and looked at the rabbit. The rabbit did indeed have beautiful soft fur. And the bird did have a beautiful voice. And the swan did have beautiful white feathers!

"You don't need to compare yourself to anybody else, Mr. Swan. Everyone is beautiful. Accept everybody just how they are. It is silly to compare yourself to the bird in the tree or to me, a rabbit, because we are not the same. You are a blessing just how you are, just like we are all blessings!"

The swan smiled and agreed. How could he compare himself to a bird or a rabbit when he was a swan? He was himself and beautiful in his own way! And so, the rabbit went on with his travels, and the swan didn't compare himself with anyone else again.

Story Two – The Way of the Fish

Across the world, there was once a great lake that was filled with all kinds of creatures and animals. There were swans and bugs that roamed around the top. Frogs came and went throughout the year to lay their eggs and raise their families. All the animals in the surrounding area came down to drink from the shoreline.

However, even though there were so many animals living in the great lake, there were only three fish. A blue fish. A red fish. And a green fish.

These three fish grew up together since they were very small and had b
friends all their lives. They would eat together, dance together in the mo
and swim together. When it was a full moon, all three fish would go to the very
bottom of the lake and swim as fast as they could up to the top and fly into the air
before falling back into the water, much to the surprise of the animals sleeping at
the time.

Life was good for the fish, and everything was peaceful.

However, one day, the blue fish was swimming around the outside of the pond
when it saw a strange-looking creature.

"Oh no," the blue fish said to himself, "that's a human being."

The blue fish crept up to the shore and put a little bit of his face out of the water
to listen.

"What an amazing lake!" the man said out loud, "I wonder how many fish I could
catch with my fishing rod here. I shall come back tomorrow and find out!"

The man left. The blue fish was scared. If the man comes back tomorrow with his
fishing rod, he could catch us all. I need to tell red fish and green fish, he thought
to himself, and swam as fast as he could across the lake to find them.

"Friends! I need to tell you something," the blue fish shouted as he found the other
two fish having breakfast.

"What is the matter?" said the red fish.

"There is a man. A human being. He is coming tomorrow to fish in the lake and to
try and catch us!"

"Oh no, what are we going to do?" the red fish asked.

Now, the blue fish was a very wise fish and would often go and speak to the other animals around the edge of the lake. He knew there was another lake not far, and if the three fish could get to this lake, then they could be safe from the fisherman.

"We can go to the other lake," the blue fish said. "If we go now when the fisherman comes tomorrow, we can be safe, and he won't catch us."

"Yes. That sounds like the best idea!" the red fish said, happy that his friend was looking out for him. Blue fish always had the best plans.

"What about you, green fish? Are you ready to go?"

The green fish sat and thought for a moment.

"No. I am not coming." He said finally.

"What?" said the red fish. "Why not?"

"Because I have lived here all my life, and I have never seen any danger. I do not believe that leaving this lake is a good idea, and I think you are both cowards for wanting to leave."

"Please come with us, green fish," the blue fish begged. "I just want us to be safe."

"No. I shall stay here." the green fish said sternly. The green fish then turned his back to the blue and red fish and swam off back to his house.

Blue fish and red fish were sad that they couldn't convince their friend to come with them, but time was running out, and they had to go.

The two fish swam to the shore and asked a big bird to carry them across the land to the other lake as quickly as possible. The bird agreed and took them across one at a time. By the evening, the two fish had settled into their new home.

The next day, the two fish watched as the fisherman turned up early in the morning and cast his fishing rod into the water. Eventually, they saw the green fish get caught by the fisherman and taken away. The fish were sad that their friend didn't listen to their warnings.

"Why did the green fish not listen and come with us? The red fish asked the blue fish.

"Because some people like to ignore their problems," said the blue fish. "When faced with a problem, you need to do something to fix the problem, not ignore it. Every problem you face in life will be different and will need a different answer, but ignoring the problem is the worst thing you can do."

Story Three – The Girl Who Wanted Happiness

There once lived a girl who lived in a big city. She lived a normal life. She went to school and saw her friends every day. She was happy, but she was not totally happy. She felt as though something in her life was not right, and she wanted more. She always thought that something was missing.

One day, she was in the school library and read about the Great Princess of the West. This princess had a castle in the mountains and was told to have the most amazing palace and held the most amazing parties that people from around the world travelled to attend. However, and most interestingly to the girl, the book said that she knew the secret to happiness.

Inspired and wanting to understand the secret of how to be happy, the girl packed her bags and left to find the Great Princess of the West.

The journey was long and tiring. The girl passed through many cities and towns. She walked through many jungles and climbed many mountains. Eventually, she crossed over the top of one mountain and there, on the other side of the valley, was the most beautiful palace she had ever seen!

"Wow! That must be where the princess lives!" the girl said to herself and set off towards it as fast as she could.

It took the girl several days to arrive at the palace, but when she arrived, there was greeted by the biggest party she had ever seen when she did. There must have been hundreds of people, all dressed in the most amazing costumes, and every table filled with the most amazing-looking food.

The palace looked amazing, and every wall and ceiling was covered in paintings and banners and decorations. However, the girl ignored it all. She went through the party, pushing through all the people and making her way across the dance floor.

Some of the partygoers wanted her to join in with the dancing, and the others offered her some of the amazing food, but she ignored them all. She had a mission to complete

After searching high and low, the girl eventually found the princess. She was dancing on the highest floor of the palace to some beautiful music that the girl had never heard before. The girl watched the princess glide across the floor in the most beautiful way and saw her smile. It was the happiest smile the girl had ever seen.

The girl waited patiently for the princess to finish dancing. When she did, the princess sat down on a large cushion on the floor and started to drink from a golden cup. The girl moved in to speak with her.

"Hello, princess. You don't know me, but I was wondering if I could talk to you."

"Of course, my child. Come and sit with me. Would you like some food?" The princess held out a silver platter that held food the girl had never seen. It smelt amazing, but the girl declined.

"What brings you to my palace? Are you enjoying the party?" The princess asked.

"I have not been to the party. I have come to ask you a question."

"Of course. What's your question, and I will see if I can help you."

"Well, I was wondering, what is the secret to happiness?"

"Ah." The princess said. "The secret to happiness is what you want to know?"

The girl nodded. The princess laughed.

"You know, this is the question everybody wants to know?"

The girl nodded.

"I have a very simple answer, and I will tell you. But first, you need to do something for me."

The girl nodded. "Yes. I will do anything to know the answer."

"Very well," said the princess.

The princess then picked up the most beautiful golden spoon from the table and handed it to the girl. She then took a bottle off the table full of purple liquid and poured a few drops into the spoon.

"Here," the princess says. "I want you to walk around the palace, go through the party and go into every room. Go everywhere and then come back to me, but make sure you don't spill a single drop from your spoon. If you can do this, then I will tell you the secret to happiness."

The girl was so happy that she was about to find out the secret. She took the spoon very carefully, making sure not to spill a single drop. She made her way through the palace, never taking her eyes off the spoon.

She moved through the party and through every room. Some rooms were really busy and were full of people, which made it really hard to keep her spoon balanced and not spill a drop.

Other rooms were really quiet and were either empty or had a few people sleeping. The girl even went outside and around the gardens, making sure she covered every single area of the palace, but never once taking her eyes off the spoon.

The palace was so big, and it took the girl all day to get around the palace and then to finally go all the way back up to the top floor to see the princess. She arrived, and the princess told her to come back and see her the next day.

The next morning, the girl went back to the princess and said,

"Princess. I took the spoon all around the palace, and I never spilled a single drop. Will you now tell me the secret to happiness?"

The princess laughed. "I will," she said, "but first you must tell me, what did you think of my wonderful palace?"

The girl stopped and thought for a moment. She had been around the entire palace, but she hadn't seen a thing. The girl didn't know how to respond. The princess picked up the spoon off the table, filled it with the purple liquid, and gave it back to the girl.

"Go around the palace again, but this time, don't think about the spoon. Just look at the palace and see everything it has to offer. Enjoy my home."

The girl nodded and set off. Not looking at the spoon, she walked around the palace and took in everything she could see. Everything was so beautiful. The artwork and the paintings were unlike anything she had ever seen.

When she reached the party, she danced with the people and ate the amazing food. She went up to the quiet rooms and looked at all the amazing books on the shelf and the stunning carpets with their stunning patterns.

She went out into the garden and ran around on the grass and smelled all the pretty flowers. Bees came up to her, and she allowed them to rest on her finger.

Eventually, after hours of enjoying the palace, the girl found herself back in the princess's room.

"Ah, there you are," the princess said as the girl entered the room, still wide-eyed with amazement at how the roof had been painted. "You've been gone for hours!"

"Yes. I am sorry. Your palace is so big and beautiful! There's so much to see and do!"

"There is indeed," said the princess. "And your spoon? Did you spill anything?"

The girl, who had completely forgotten about the spoon since she was having so much fun exploring the palace, held it out. It was empty, and all the liquid had been spilled.

"Ah," said the princess. "Do you see the secret to happiness now?"

The girl shook her head.

"You see, if you go through your life only looking at one thing in your life, you may be able to hold onto it and never it go, but you'll miss all the beautiful and amazing things around you. What bought you more happiness? The spoon or the palace?"

"The palace!" squealed the girl, "The palace is amazing!"

"Then, as you go through your life, always look around you at the beautiful things in front of you. Find joy and beauty in everything that is offered to you, rather than focusing on the things like the spoon that don't really matter."

Story Four – The Boy Who Cried Wolf

There was once a small boy who lived in a village with his parents. The village was very quiet, and nothing really happened. Every day was the same and, as the boy was growing up, he found himself getting more and more bored.

His father, who was a shepherd that looked after the village's sheep, told his son that he needed help. He said to go up the hill and watch the sheep to make sure they are safe while they graze in the fields and get home safely to the farm at night.

The boy agreed because he had nothing better to do, so off he went to the fields. He went every single day and sat on the edge of the hill. He watched the sheep go all the way to one side of the field and then all the way back again. Most days he would sleep, but then his father caught him and would poke him with a stick until he woke up.

One day, however, he thought of a funny idea.

He stood up and ran all the way back down the hill in a panic, throwing his arms into the air while he screamed. When he reached the village, everybody was looking at him out of their windows and doors. His father ran down the street to meet him.

"Son? Are you okay? What has happened?" his father said, trying to calm his son down.

"There's⋯ there's... there's a wolf in the field with the sheep!"

Everybody panicked. The mothers with their children ran into their houses and locked the doors. The men grabbed pitchforks and spears and marched off to the field to scare off the wolf. The boy watched and followed, trying not to laugh to himself.

When they reached the field, the men searched high and low for the wolf, but of course, the boy was lying, so they did not find a wolf.

"Where did you see the wolf, son?"

"I think it was over there," he said, pointing towards the big hill he had sat on for weeks. The men searched over the hill and all around the area until the daytime turned to night-time, but still, they found no wolf.

They searched hard because the sheep were so important to the village. They provided them with food and wool for making clothes and selling to passing traders, so they could not afford to lose a single one.

The men and the boy returned to the village, and everyone relaxed, believing that the wolf must have seen everyone coming and ran away.

The next day, the boy was sat back on the hill and found himself bored again. He kept thinking about the day before and how much fun it had been to see everyone running around and hunting down a wolf that didn't exist. He decided to do it all over again, just for a joke.

Just like the day before, the boy ran down the hill and back into the village, screaming at the top of his voice,

"Help! Help! The wolf has come back, and the sheep are in danger!"

And, just like the day before, all the mothers took their children into the houses and locked the doors, and the men took their weapons and pitchforks and marched up to the sheep field.

And, just like the day before, the men searched high and low for the wolf but found not a single paw print in the dirt. When it was night, the men took the sheep back to the farm and settled in for the evening. Everyone was sad because they had spent all their time looking for a wolf for the last two days, and now they were behind on all the jobs that needed to be done in the village, like building huts and making fires.

That night, when the shepherd farmer was putting his son to be, he sat down on the edge of the bed and asked him a question.

"Son," he said, "I know it can be boring sitting up there on the hill watching over the sheep, but it's such a big responsibility that needs to be done. You know that, right?"

"Of course, father. I know that."

"And you know that if you are lying about the wolf, this can make bad things happen?"

"I know, dad." The boy said, and the family went off to sleep.

The next day the boy went up to the field and was thinking about what his father had said. He sat on the hill and started watching the sheep and found himself bored almost straight away.

"Ah, well," the boy thought to himself. "All the fun and excitement of hunting the last few days have made my day! One more day can't hurt."

As the boy stood up to run down the hill, a grey blur caught his eye. There, right on the outskirts of the sheep field, was a wolf sneaking up on the sheep. It was the biggest, meanest, most scary-looking wolf the boy had ever seen! He couldn't even dream of a scarier looking wolf!

Full of terror and panic, the boy ran down the hill and back to the village as fast as he could! He screamed with his arms in the air.

"Please! Come, help me! There is a wolf in the field with the sheep, and it's going to eat them all!"

However, this time the village did not panic. The mothers and their children looked at the boy and shook their heads before carrying on with what they were doing before.

The men, who were making fires and fixing the huts, ignored the boy and carried on with the work they were doing.

The boy's father came out of his house and stroked his boy's head.

"I'm sorry, son. If you lie, then nobody is going to believe you. Now go back up to the sheep field and look after them. We'll see you at dinner time when we come and get the sheep back in."

The boy, with tears in his eyes, begged and pleaded with his father to come and help him with the wolf, but the father just told him to go back and stop wasting everyone's time.

Story Five – The Greedy Man

Far away on the other side of the world, and a long time ago, there lived a man in a small town. This man was plagued by the sin of greed, and no matter what he had in life, he always wanted more.

When he grew up and started to earn money, he would always want more, even if this meant he had to steal it. When he was eating with his family, he would always have the biggest plate and would even hide food so he could have more later. He always wanted more, and he didn't care if other people missed out.

One day, the man was walking on the outskirts of town among the trees and the bushes when he heard a cry for help.

"Help me. Please. I need someone to help!" The man, confused by what the cries for help could be, looked high and low for the sound and where it was coming from. Eventually, he came across a large bush covered with thorns and berries. There, in the bush, tangled among the branches, he saw a small fairy.

"Ah, I'm so glad you're here, stranger," said the fairy, "I've been trapped in this bush for hours and haven't been able to get out. Can you help me?"

The man nodded and stepped forward to help. He was quite bewildered as he had never seen a fairy in real life before. He had only ever heard about them in stories as he was growing up and in the fairy tales his mother used to tell him.

However, just as he was about to free the fairy, he remembered his mother telling him that fairies were magical creatures and could cast magical spells. The man stopped and took a step back.

"Now see here, magical fairy," the man exclaimed boldly. "You are a fairy with magical powers, am I right?"

"You are right, indeed, sir."

"Well then, I will only free you if you promise to grant me one wish for helping you."

"But sir. My wand is tangled in the bush, too, and I can't wave it."

"Promise me the wish, and I will free you." The man said. His eyes were wide as ever as he thought of all the wealth and riches he could get from the wish that could be coming.

"I promise I will grant you one wish you if you free me."

The man gave a little squeal of excitement and thought about everything he could wish for that could make him the richest, wealthiest, and happiness man on the planet. He untangled the branches that trapped the fairy and stepped back.

The fairy was beautiful and opened her wings and started hovering just above the man.

"Thank you so much," said the fairy. "I thought I would have to stay there all day and all night in the cold."

"Yes. Yes," said the man. He didn't care what the fairy had to say. "Just give me my wish, please. You promised." The fairy shook her head, disappointed.

"I will grant you the wish because I promised I would, but remember, in life, you don't need to get as much as you can from other people, but rather you can help and look out for people without being greedy. If you do this, you will find riches and happiness beyond anything you can imagine. Greed will always come back to get you."

"Please. Just give me my wish." The man begged. He wasn't listening to the fairy and her warnings. His mind was full of images of gold and jewels.

"Very well," said the fairy. "What is your wish?"

"I wish that whatever I touched turned to gold." The man said. His eyes were so wide, and he couldn't believe he was about to have as much gold as he wanted.

"Very well." The fairy flicked her wand, and golden sparkles flew out of the end and wrapped themselves around the man. He watched as the glitter sparkled in front of him and then faded away into nothing.

The man wasn't sure if the spell had worked. The fairy just stood hovering in the air, watching the man, waiting for him to say thank you, but he never did.

The man looked at his hands. There were no markings or anything different about them.

"Did it work?" he asked the fairy.

"See for yourself," she said back.

The man bent down and touched a stone that was lying on the ground. As soon as his finger touched it, it turned into solid, shiny gold. He picked up the stone and examined it. It was real gold! He now had the power to become as rich and as wealthy as he wanted!

The man took off into the woods and back into the town, leaving the fairy behind without even saying goodbye. As the man ran, he touched stones and trees and bushes, turning them all into gold.

He ran through the town and into his house, and there his daughter was sitting at the kitchen table.

"You'll never guess what, daughter!" he laughed so loudly. "We're going to be so rich we'll never have to worry about money ever again!"

As he said this, he bent down and went to pick his daughter up to hug her, but of course, the moment he touched her with his hands, she turned into a solid gold statue. He tried over and over again to bring her back to life and to reverse the spell, but he didn't know-how.

And so, for the rest of his life, the man traveled the world, never touching anything or hugging anyone, never even holding hands with someone, as he tried to find the fairy to undo the spell. He was forever sad his greed had made him lose everything that was special to him.

Story Six – The Boy on Sports Day

There once was a boy called Ben, who went to a normal school and lived in a normal town. He was a typical boy who went to classes and had a group of friends that he played football with. He got normal grades and had a pretty normal life.

One year at school, the headteacher came into the classroom and said,

"Hello everybody. This year we are going to be holding a sports day for everyone, and everyone must attend."

Some children looked very happy. They were good at sports and loved to come first place in all the races and sports they played in. Other children, including Ben, weren't so happy because they weren't as good at sports as the other children and knew they were going to lose.

Ben went home that night and spoke to his mother.

"Mum, I don't want to play in the sports day. All the other kids are better than me, and I'm going to lose."

"When you do anything in life," his mother replied, "it's not about winning or losing; it's about trying your hardest and doing the best you can do as a person, not comparing yourself to what everyone else can do."

"But I don't want to lose."

"But if you don't try and you don't do anything, then you've already lost."

The boy understood what his mother was saying. It doesn't matter if you win or lose. What matters is doing the best, no matter what. If you can do this, you'll always be a winner to yourself.

And so, the boy took his mother's advice and started to practice hard. The boy got up early and ran every morning before school and would exercise after school. He made sure he ate the right food and didn't eat too much. He practiced harder and harder, and eventually; the sports day arrived.

It was a beautiful day, and everybody in school came to the big sports field with their parents. The boy and his mother arrived, and his mother took a seat in the crowd to watch.

The boy watched with his classmates as the other classes did their runs. Some kids were really fast and won their races easily. Some kids fell over and hurt themselves. Some kids cried when they lost and ran over to their parents.

Eventually, the headteacher stood up and said it was Ben's class turn to run in the races.

Ben and the other kids lined up on the racetrack and got ready to run. Ben forgot about everything and everyone. He just wanted to run like he had been practicing. It wasn't a race. It was just like running at home on his own.

Ben heard the starting whistle, and he ran. He took off so fast and pushed himself faster and faster. As he got near the end of the finish line, he took a little look to his left and to his right and didn't see the other kids.

"Oh no," Ben thought to himself, "The other kids have already finished. I've lost."

While Ben knew it wasn't about winning or losing, he still felt bad he had lost. Even so, he pushed to go faster and made it over the finish line. He didn't care that he lost. He just was just happy that he did his best.

Once he went over the line, he turned to find his mother in the crowd. However, much to Ben's surprise, the other children were still running down the track. Ben looked around him and realized he had finished first!

The other children finished, even the faster sporty kids had finished after Ben! The headteacher came over and gave him the gold medal for coming first and shook the hands of all the other children who ran.

He then went over to his mother, happier than ever before, excited to show her his medal!

"Look, mom," he said, "I won the race!"

"See," his mother said, stroking his head and smiling at him. "You put the hard work in and didn't focus on everyone else, but you focused on yourself, and you managed to be the best! Did you have fun?"

"Yes, it wasn't about winning or losing. I just did the best I could!"

Story Seven – The Struggling Pebble

High up in the mountains of a mystical land, there was the widest, most beautiful lake anybody had ever seen. The water came straight off the mountain and was ice cold but completely clear, so you could see the riverbed.

Along the river, there were beautiful trees that had guarded the riverbank for hundreds of years, and all the animals in the area came down to the river to drink and wash because the waters were so refreshing.

However, one of the most unlikely creatures to live in this magical river was a pebble. The pebble was just like any other pebble. It was round and grey and sat with the rest of the pebbles and spent all day letting the river water wash over them in the most relaxing way.

For the pebble, life was perfect. He would spend all day talking with the other pebbles and chatting with any animals that came to the river to wash and drink. He spent all his life in the river, and it was truly the place the pebble called home.

However, one fateful day, there was a storm up in the mountains, and all the rainwater came down and made the river flow so fast. All the animals ran from the river, and all the pebbles and stones held onto the riverbank as far as much as they could. However, this one little pebble couldn't hold on, and there was a big whoosh of current, and the pebble was picked up and carried down the river!

The pebble tried as hard as it could to hold on, bumping itself into other pebbles and the riverbed to try and not move, but the water was flowing too fast, and the current was too strong!

Eventually, the storm settled and the pebble came to rest on the riverbed, but this was not the pebble's home. The pebble floated over to the shore, and there he found a moose, drinking from the side.

"Hello moose," the pebble said, "Do you know where I am?"

"Why yes, little pebble," the moose replied, "You're in the river!"

"Very funny," said the pebble. "Please, I need to get back home."

"Well, I don't know where your home is, but I know that this is the world. Look around at how beautiful it all is."

"No, thank you," said the pebble. "Thank you for your time, though." The moose nodded as the pebble pushed away from the shore of the river and back in. I must get home, the pebble thought to itself.

With all its might, the pebble pushed into the river and tried to float upstream, but the more effort the pebble put in to move, the less it moved. The pebble tried so hard to move upstream, but it simply didn't work.

The pebble, lost and confused, tried for hours to push and push against the current of the river but still couldn't move. Minutes turned to hours, and the pebble found itself even further downstream than when it had started. Through all the struggling, the pebble didn't even notice a small crayfish had come out of hiding and was watching the pebble push.

"Are you okay there, little pebble?" the crayfish said. "You look very tired."

"No. I'm not okay. I'm lost, and I need to get home."

"Well, you know you're never going to get home pushing against the current," said the crayfish. "Life is all about letting go and going with the flow. That's how you see what is most beautiful in life."

"No. I need to get home."

"But look around little pebble. What do you see?"

The pebble looked around. It was nearly night-time at this point in the day and was starting to get dark. However, unlike where the pebble lived, there weren't as many trees here, only vast fields that stretched out as far as the pebble could see.

And, at this time of day, there was the most beautiful sunset that filled the sky with orange and pink colors and made everything look so beautiful. However, the pebble was so caught up with the thoughts in its head; it saw nothing.

"No, I must go," said the pebble, and it pushed off into the current to carry on down the stream.

"Suit yourself," said the crayfish. "Don't forget to go with the flow!"

That night, the pebble couldn't sleep. He just drifted further and further down the stream, and there was no hope of it getting home. However, the crayfish's words played over and over again in the pebble's head.

Go with the flow. Go with the flow. What did that silly crayfish mean? Go with the flow? Like the flow in the river.

The pebble tried to relax and 'go with the flow,' and when it did, the most extraordinary thing happened. The pebble started to have fun.

As the current and waters of the river twisted and turned down the hill, the pebble 'whooped' and 'ahhed' with every bump. Sometimes, the pebble would get so much speed it would fly out of the water and crash back down with an almighty splash that made the pebble laugh so much.

Even though it was night-time, lots of other pebbles woke up along the way and saw how much fun the pebble was having, and some even decided to join in! Before the pebble knew it, there were dozens of pebbles floating down the river having the best time of their lives! At one point, even the salmon jumped in, much to the amazement of all the animals on the shore.

Hours went by, and eventually, the pebble was so very tired. It stopped bouncing and having fun in the water and just relaxed and let the current push him down. Eventually, the currents of the river died away, and the water here was still and calm. The sun was just coming up across the horizon. It was morning.

Just as the pebble was catching its breath, it noticed a huge shape moving underneath it in the water. The pebble was scared, as it couldn't see the riverbed anymore, or not even any ground. The water just went on and on forever.

"Hello there, little pebble," a booming voice called out from the depths of the water. "What are you doing this far out of your home?"

In an instant, a huge whale appeared in front of the pebble.

"I'm sorry, whale," the pebble started, "I'm just going with the flow and ended up here. Where exactly is here?"

"You're in the ocean, little pebble' the whale replied. "And what do you mean, going with the flow?"

"Well, I live in a river, but a storm happened and pushed me out of my home and down the river. I tried so hard to get back, but I couldn't do it, so I did what the crayfish told me to do and just floated down. I've had the most amazing time!"

The whale found it all very hard to believe.

"I will show you," the pebble said, and asked the whale to take the pebble to the surface of the ocean.

It was unlike anything the pebble had ever seen before. There was so much water and no banks, riverbeds, or shorelines. Just water as far as the pebble could see. With the sun coming up and reflecting off the surface, the pebble sighed as it had never seen anything more beautiful in all its life.

"You see Mr. Whale. This place is so beautiful. If I was just focusing on one thing and living in my head with my thoughts, I would never be able to see the world for how beautiful it is. I just had to relax and go with the flow!"

The whale took a deep breath and closed its eyes, so deep that the pebble thought it was going to get sucked inside the whale, but it was okay. The whale then breathed out and opened its eyes again and saw its home in a whole new light.

"You are right, little pebble. This is such a beautiful place, and I only don't notice that it's beautiful because I see it every day. Thank you for sharing your wisdom with me."

And so, the pebble traveled the currents of the oceans, exploring all it could find and going wherever nature took it, and sharing the crayfish's message with it wherever it went, showing the world to relax and just go with the flow, rather than spending all their energy trying to fight the current.

Story Eight – The Desert Rose Garden

There once existed a garden that was owned by a wizard who could be only be found in the hottest desert in the world. There was a magical rose within the garden that the wizard had cast a spell on, making the rose the most beautiful rose in all the garden.

"Everyone. Look. Another day you get to see me and how beautiful I am," said the rose. The rose then proceeded to dance in the wind, twisting and turning and making sure every single petal reflected the dazzling desert sunlight.

All the other flowers and plants looked in wonder and wished that one day they too could be as beautiful as the rose.

Another plant in the garden that happened to be planted right next to the rose was a cactus.

The cactus had been in the garden for hundreds of years and stood proud and tall of itself. Every day, the rose would wake up from the night and would insult the cactus standing tall.

"Haha!" the rose would say. "Look at you with your spikes and your greenness and your nothing-much-else. You call yourself a plant? Where are your petals? Your flowers are so white and small. Not like the beautiful red that I am."

The cactus did not respond.

Day in, day out, the rose would dance in the wind and laugh about how much prettier it was than the cactus. The other flowers said nothing in return, for they were scared the rose would turn around insult them instead!

However, the tables were about to turn.

One summer, the wizard, who had gone to visit the rose and his garden every single day to look after and water them, for it was a desert in which he lived, set off on an adventure. He had to go to the Great Library to file some books away that were to be kept there.

Yet, when he left, he forgot to put a spell on all the plants so that they would stay watered and healthy. The wizard was gone for days, and then for weeks, and then they turned into months.

Being so beautiful, the rose had been given a flowerpot all to itself, and so for many weeks, the rose survived like normal. However, one day, a desert sandstorm rolled in, as did one of the hottest summers the desert had seen in many centuries.

The rose became battered and bruised in the sandstorm, and once the sandstorm had vanished, the heat dried up the tank of water, and the rose was left dry.

"Please," the rose said as its once beautiful petals started to wilt in the dry heat. "Please, can someone help me? I think I'm going to die."

The cactus, who had been watching the rose this whole time, approached the rose and said,

"Why, of course, Rose. I can help you. As you know, cacti are masters at surviving in the desert, and we store water inside ourselves, so here. Take some of mine."

The rose was incredibly grateful to the cactus for helping it.

"But why? All these years, I've been so horrible to you about how you look. Why would you choose to help me?"

"Because," said the cactus, in his usual booming voice that sounded so full of wisdom, "Being beautiful isn't about what you look like, either to yourself or to other people. It's about the kind of person you are on the inside."

"But I've been ugly on the inside," said the rose.

"It doesn't matter, little rose. Everybody can forgive and grow together. Be beautiful on the inside, and this is what people will see."

From that moment on, the little rose decided to be so beautiful and kind on the inside, and the garden was united as one.

Disclaimer

This book contains opinions and ideas of the author and is meant to teach the reader informative and helpful knowledge while due care should be taken by the user in the application of the information provided. The instructions and strategies are possibly not right for every reader and there is no guarantee that they work for everyone. Using this book and implementing the information/recipes therein contained is explicitly your own responsibility and risk. This work with all its contents, does not guarantee correctness, completion, quality or correctness of the provided information. Misinformation or misprints cannot be completely eliminated.

Printed in Great Britain
by Amazon